'Don't let fear hold you back.
You're **braver** than you think!'

Join Kitty for an **enchanting**
adventure by the light of the **moon**.

Kitty can **talk to animals** and
has **feline superpowers**.

Meet Kitty & her Cat Crew

Kitty

Kitty has special powers, but is she ready to be a superhero just like her mum?

Luckily Kitty's Cat Crew have faith in her and show Kitty the hero that lies within!

Pumpkin

A stray ginger kitten who is utterly devoted to Kitty.

Figaro

Excitable and ready for adventure, Figaro knows
the neighbourhood like the back of his paw.

Pixie

Pixie has a nose for trouble
and a very active imagination!

Katsumi

Sleek and sophisticated,
Katsumi is quick to call Kitty
at the first sign of trouble.

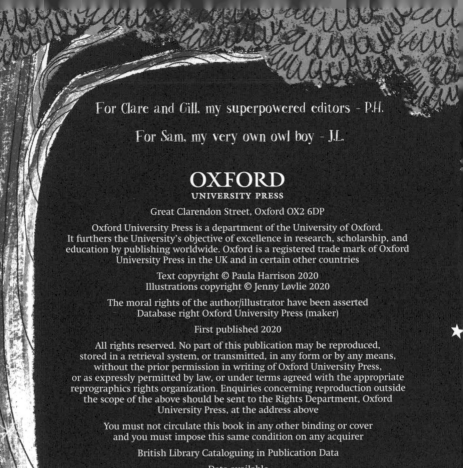

For Clare and Gill, my superpowered editors – P.H.

For Sam, my very own owl boy – J.L.

OXFORD
UNIVERSITY PRESS

Great Clarendon Street, Oxford OX2 6DP

Oxford University Press is a department of the University of Oxford.
It furthers the University's objective of excellence in research, scholarship, and
education by publishing worldwide. Oxford is a registered trade mark of Oxford
University Press in the UK and in certain other countries

First published 2020

British Library Cataloguing in Publication Data

Data available

ISBN: 978-0-19-277168-1

1 3 5 7 9 10 8 6 4 2

Printed in China

Paper used in the production of this book is a natural,
recyclable product made from wood grown in sustainable forests.
The manufacturing process conforms to the environmental
regulations of the country of origin.

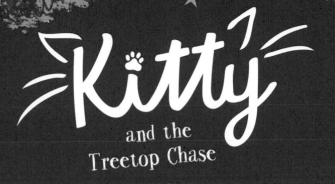

Kitty

and the
Treetop Chase

OXFORD
UNIVERSITY PRESS

Chapter
1

'There you are, Pumpkin!
That looks just like you.' Kitty drew the
last whisker on to her cat picture and
showed it to Pumpkin.

She had drawn a plump little ginger
cat with bright eyes and a stripy tail.

Pumpkin jumped onto the table to take a closer look. 'It's me!' he purred, rubbing his furry head against Kitty's arm. 'I really like it.'

'I'll put it up on the wall,' said Kitty, smiling.

She and Pumpkin had been best friends ever since she'd rescued him from a tall clock tower. Kitty had cat-like superpowers and she was learning to become a real superhero. Sometimes she went on adventures in the moonlight with her cat crew. She loved climbing and balancing on the rooftops, and using her special night-time vision and super hearing to spot when trouble was coming.

Most of all, Kitty loved being able to talk to animals, and especially to

Pumpkin, who was the sweetest kitten in the world!

Kitty stuck the picture of Pumpkin on the wall and stood back to admire it. Then she noticed a delicious scent drifting out of the kitchen. Pumpkin's nose started twitching too.

'That smells lovely!' said Kitty. 'I wonder if Mum's doing some baking.'

She ran into the kitchen, where Mum was taking a large cake tin out of the oven. 'Have you made a cake? Mmm . . . smells like chocolate!'

'There's nothing wrong with your super senses!' laughed Mum. 'Yes, I've made a special cake because we have visitors coming to stay tonight.

Some very good friends have just moved to Hallam City and they have a son who's your age.'

'Oh! What's his name?' asked Kitty.

Mum lifted the cake out of the cake tin and a cloud of chocolatey steam filled the kitchen. 'He's called Ozzy. You could have a sleepover in the new tree house if you like.' She gave Kitty a funny smile. 'I'm sure you'll find you have a lot in common.'

Kitty hesitated. Dad had built the tree house in the garden last week, and it was meant to belong to her as her brother, Max, was too young to be allowed up the ladder on his own. She wasn't sure she wanted to share it with anyone else.

Ding-dong went the doorbell.

'That must be them now!' Kitty's mum put down the oven gloves. 'I hope they're hungry.'

Kitty's forehead wrinkled as her mum hurried to the door.

Why had her mum said she might have a lot in common with Ozzy? It seemed strange when she'd never met him before!

Kitty's mum called to her from the hall. 'Kitty, come and meet everyone! These are my friends Molly and Neil Porter, and this is Ozzy.' She pointed to a boy with curly dark hair and round glasses.

Kitty said hello

while Pumpkin hid behind her legs. The
Porters said hello back and smiled in
a friendly way, but Ozzy just nodded
awkwardly and fiddled with his glasses.

'Why don't you show everyone
around, Kitty?' said her dad, coming
into the hall. 'Max and I will set the
dinner table.'

Kitty showed the Porters around
the house and they said how much
they liked her room before asking
her all about her school. Ozzy just
followed them from room to room and

didn't say a thing.

'This is terrible!' Kitty whispered
to Pumpkin. 'What if he doesn't speak
for the whole sleepover?'

Pumpkin put his paw on Kitty's
knee. 'Don't worry,' he whispered back.
'I'll keep you company.'

After they'd eaten dinner and had
a slice of the chocolate cake, Kitty's
mum turned to Ozzy with a smile.
'I thought it might be lovely for you
and Kitty to have your sleepover in the
tree house tonight. It's so much more

exciting than sleeping indoors!'

'I can show you if you like,' added
Kitty, jumping up from the table.

Ozzy followed Kitty out of the
back door into the shadowy garden.
Moonlight glinted on the windows
and the silver watering can. The round
garden lights cast a soft yellow glow
across the flower beds, and a tiny breath
of wind made the flowers sway and the
trees rustle.

Kitty's dad had built the tree house
in the big oak tree at the far end of the

garden. A sturdy wooden ladder led
up into the branches. Ozzy and Kitty
climbed the rungs in silence.

'Here it is. I hope you like it!' Kitty
clambered into the little wooden house.

The place was quite
roomy and she had set
pots of marigolds on the
windowsills and hung a
mobile of glittery stars from
the roof to make it pretty.

Ozzy looked all around, blinking as
he peered up at the starry mobile.

Kitty wondered if he felt nervous
about sleeping outside. 'We don't have
to sleep here if you don't want to. I
know not everyone likes being outside
in the dark . . .'

'I love being outside in the dark!'
said Ozzy, his eyes lighting up suddenly.
'Everything looks more interesting at
night.'

Kitty looked at him in surprise.
At least he was talking to her at last!

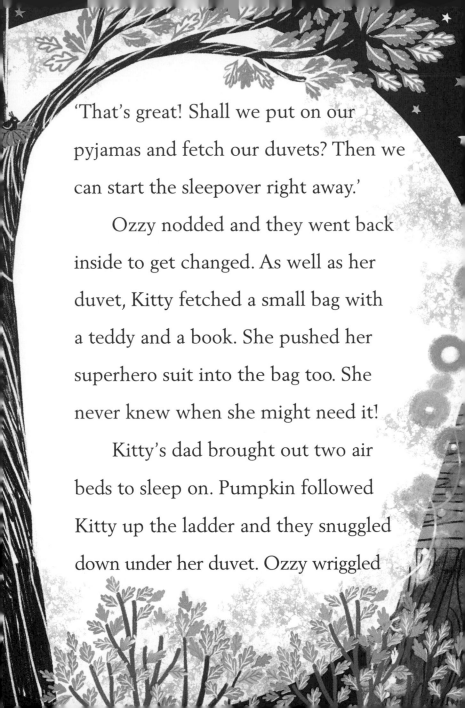

'That's great! Shall we put on our
pyjamas and fetch our duvets? Then we
can start the sleepover right away.'

Ozzy nodded and they went back
inside to get changed. As well as her
duvet, Kitty fetched a small bag with
a teddy and a book. She pushed her
superhero suit into the bag too. She
never knew when she might need it!

Kitty's dad brought out two air
beds to sleep on. Pumpkin followed
Kitty up the ladder and they snuggled
down under her duvet. Ozzy wriggled

down under his own duvet and stared
around with wide, dark eyes.

Kitty gazed out of the tree
house window at the moonlit garden.

Her cat-like night vision allowed her to
see everything so clearly. Stars twinkled
across the deep black sky, and a wisp
of smoke curled out of next-door's
chimney.

'It feels magical when there's a full
moon, doesn't it?' Kitty said.

Ozzy nodded and lay down. 'I'm
going to sleep now. Good night!'

Kitty tried to stay awake for a little
while, although Pumpkin was already
fast asleep beside her. The wind swirled
around the garden, and the tree house

swayed gently with
the branches of the oak tree.
Kitty felt as if she was being
rocked to sleep, and at last her
eyelids drooped and she couldn't
stay awake any more.

Chapter 2

Kitty woke to a tapping
noise on the tree house window. She
sat up, sleepily pushing her hair away
from her face. It must be one of her cat
crew calling her to go on an adventure.
Perhaps Pixie had found a new place to

explore or maybe Figaro had come to tell her someone was in trouble.

Pumpkin yawned and pricked up his ears. 'What's that, Kitty? Is something happening?'

Kitty spotted Katsumi's honey-coloured fur and serious dark eyes outside the window. She scrambled up and undid the latch. Ozzy didn't stir so she kept her voice to a whisper. 'Hello, Katsumi. Is everything all right?'

Katsumi sprang inside, her tail swaying. 'There's a commotion at the bakery. The bakery owners got a new dog not long ago and he's bounding up and down, absolutely wrecking the place! I think we should go over there and stop him.'

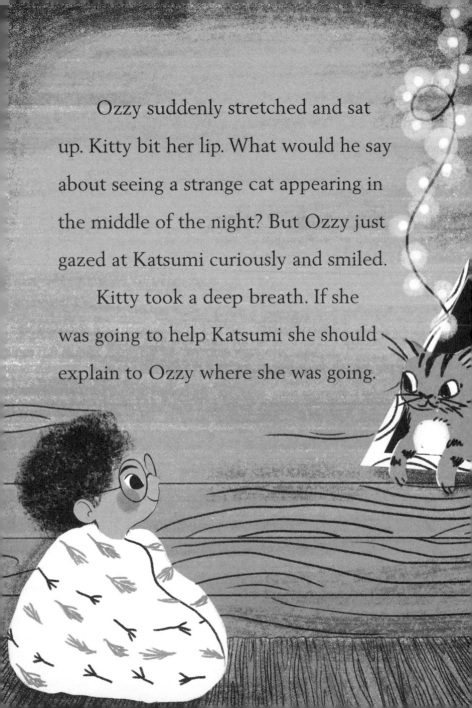

Ozzy suddenly stretched and sat up. Kitty bit her lip. What would he say about seeing a strange cat appearing in the middle of the night? But Ozzy just gazed at Katsumi curiously and smiled.

Kitty took a deep breath. If she was going to help Katsumi she should explain to Ozzy where she was going.

'Um . . . I have something to tell you. I'm a superhero with cat-like powers! I often go on adventures in the moonlight, especially when someone needs my help. Katsumi's just told me about an emergency.'

'That's funny!' Ozzy grinned. 'I'm a superhero too.' He leaned out of the window and made a long hooting sound.

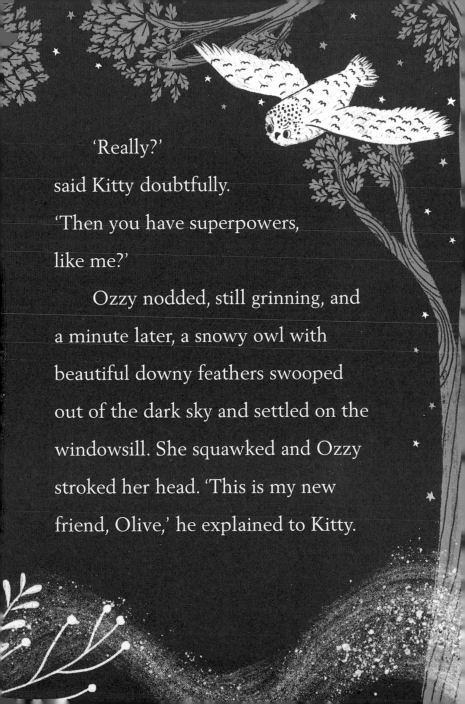

'Really?'
said Kitty doubtfully.
'Then you have superpowers,
like me?'

Ozzy nodded, still grinning, and
a minute later, a snowy owl with
beautiful downy feathers swooped
out of the dark sky and settled on the
windowsill. She squawked and Ozzy
stroked her head. 'This is my new
friend, Olive,' he explained to Kitty.

'I met her just after moving here to Hallam City.'

Kitty stared in surprise. Then she remembered she didn't want to seem rude. 'Hello, Olive. I'm Kitty and this is Pumpkin and Katsumi.'

Olive bobbed her head to each of them. 'Ozzy is training to be a superhero and his owl-like powers give him amazing eyesight and super

hearing. When he's finished his training he'll be unstoppable!' she said proudly. 'We've already had our first moonlit adventure together.'

Ozzy pulled a brown cloak lined with dark feathers from his sleepover bag. 'I wear this cape, you see! The feathers let me swoop and glide just like an owl, and they're brilliant for camouflage! I have a mask too.' He put on his superhero outfit and a feathery mask. His eyes looked big and wide as he blinked at Kitty.

Kitty hunted inside her own bag before pulling out her black cape, cat

ears, and mask. She put on her superhero outfit. For a long moment, Kitty and Ozzy stared at each other.

'Wow! A cape that lets you glide sounds great,' Kitty said at last. 'I spend a lot of time jumping and somersaulting, so I don't really need one of those.'

'Most people wouldn't be able to use it properly anyway,' Ozzy told her.

Kitty frowned. She was sure she'd manage to use a cape like that if she wanted to!

Ozzy quickly explained to Olive that there was a dog going wild in the bakery.

'I think we should hurry,' urged Katsumi. 'Who knows what this dog will do next?'

Kitty dashed to the door of the tree house with Pumpkin scampering after her. 'We can follow the rooftops. I'll show you!'

'I think it would be better to use the trees,' replied Ozzy. 'You know the way, don't you Olive?'

'Yes, follow me!' Olive flew over the fence and glided across the garden next door.

'Oh! I guess we could do that.' Kitty climbed swiftly to the top of the tree with Katsumi close behind her. She leaned down to help Pumpkin who was struggling to reach the next branch. Ozzy clambered up beside her, puffing a little.

He clutched the branches tightly,
wobbling as the tree swayed in the wind.

'Will you be all right?' Kitty felt
her superpowers growing inside her.
She knew she could easily leap to the
next tree, but would Ozzy be able to

keep up with her?

Ozzy grinned and spread out his feathered cape. 'Of course I will! Watch this.' And he leapt into the air. The wind rippled through his cloak like a sail as he silently glided to the next tree

Kitty sprang after him, landing perfectly in the treetop. Her cat-like powers tingled through her body like electricity. The jump to the next tree was even wider. Ozzy grinned at Kitty as he set off, swooping noiselessly through the air.

Kitty gathered Pumpkin into her arms. She knew the jump would be too much for the kitten. 'Hold on tight!' she whispered and Pumpkin clung to her shoulders, his stripy tail curled around her neck.

Kitty and Ozzy went on swooping and leaping from treetop to treetop. Olive flew on ahead while Katsumi leapt gracefully along the branches. The houses were dark and the back gardens were only lit by moonlight.

At last, Ozzy reached the last tree and swooped to the ground.

He landed gracefully beside a
hedge, almost camouflaged by his
cloak. Kitty sprang on to a fence
before somersaulting to land
on the pavement.

'Nice moves!' Ozzy nodded.

'Thanks—you too!' Kitty smiled.

'We're here!' Katsumi nodded to the bakery on the opposite side of the street. 'There was a terrible commotion earlier.'

Kitty gazed at the shop front, which was hung with a large pink sign: *The Sticky Bun Bakery*. She remembered coming here a few weeks ago to buy doughnuts, and the owners, Mr and Mrs Gallo, had been very friendly.

Ozzy tilted his head a little, frowning intently as he stared through the bakery's dark windows. 'It all seems quiet in there now. I think we should keep watch for a bit—see if anything happens.'

Kitty shook her head. 'We need to find out what's going on! I'll go in by myself if you want.'

Ozzy frowned. 'No way! We should both go. I'll race you there!' He darted across the silent street and Kitty ran after him. She was determined not to let him be the first one inside!

Chapter 3

Ozzy and Kitty rushed across the empty road. Katsumi and Pumpkin scampered after them, and Olive fluttered overhead. Moonlight glinted on the bakery sign and rows of cherry buns and pink-iced cupcakes

on display, close to the door. Kitty
slipped around the back and found an
open window. She climbed onto the
windowsill and peered in. It was dark
inside.

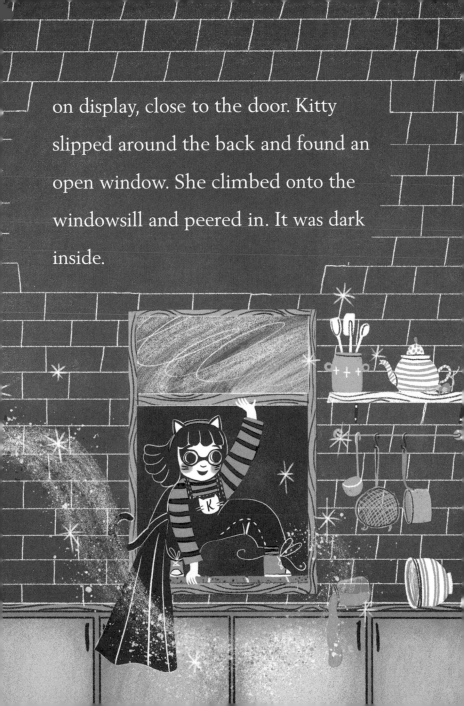

'Be careful, Kitty!' Pumpkin's tail twitched nervously.

Slipping through the window, Kitty dropped to the floor and looked around. This was the kitchen, with rows of large ovens and shelves stacked with ingredients. There was no sign of the dog, but the worktop was covered with white flour in such a thick layer it looked as though it had snowed.

One shelf had fallen down, scattering cherries and raisins all over the floor. Kitty gaped at the mess.

Why would the dog have done this to his new home?

Ozzy tapped on the door. 'Let us in, Kitty! What's going on in there?'

Kitty hurried to unlock the door, nearly tripping over an upside-down mixing bowl. 'It's even worse than I expected. It looks as if a whole pack of animals jumped around in here!'

'Maybe he was really hungry
and he was searching for dog food,'
suggested Ozzy.

'Dogs can be such messy creatures!
A bird would never do something like
this.' Olive settled on a worktop and
then clicked her beak crossly at the
flour on her talons.

'I don't think he can be a very nice dog,' said Pumpkin nervously. 'He's not lying in wait to pounce on us, is he?'

'I don't think so. Let's see if there are any clues in the shop.' Kitty dashed down the corridor and gasped. A splendid three-tier cake with swirls of lemon-coloured icing lay squashed on the floor. Katsumi, who had followed Kitty, shook her head.

'Poor Mr and Mrs Gallo! They're going to be so upset when

they see what's happened,' said Kitty. 'We'd better find this dog before he causes even more trouble.'

'There are paw prints here!' Ozzy pointed to the trail of sticky marks that led all over the shop. 'If we follow them they'll lead us straight to him.'

Kitty looked closely at the paw prints. 'It's this way!' She darted down the corridor into a store room with an odd door hatch at one end.

'This must be where they deliver the sacks of flour,' said Katsumi.

Kitty pushed the hatch and it swung open gently.

'We'll never get through there. It's too narrow,' Ozzy told her.

'I can get through! Go back through the door and I'll meet you in the yard.' Crouching low, Kitty squeezed gracefully through the hatch and out the other side. Pumpkin and Katsumi followed her, and they found themselves in a small backyard leading to a side alley.

The sticky paw prints glinted in the moonlight. The trail led across the yard and over some empty crates towards the alley.

A distant howl rose into the air and

the hairs on the back of Kitty's neck prickled. Was that the dog they were looking for? She listened carefully, but the howling stopped and a thick silence settled over the bakery backyard.

Ozzy ran out of the back door. 'Did you hear that? Sounds like this dog is still close by.'

'Such a horrible noise!' Olive shuddered as she settled on Ozzy's shoulder.

Kitty suddenly wondered if the creature was dangerous. She didn't say anything to Ozzy. He already looked nervous—blinking and fiddling with his mask. She glanced at Katsumi, Pumpkin, and Olive. 'At least there are five of us and we can look for the dog together. We'd better track him down before he causes even more damage!'

They hurried down the alley, following the trail of paw prints. The sticky prints soon faded, but Kitty spotted other clues that showed the dog had passed by. There was a patch of golden fur on a prickly bush, and a

garden gate that was marked by the
deep gash of claws. The lower branch of
a tree had been pulled off and its leaves
scattered along the pavement.

Ozzy frowned at the dark mass of trees on the other side of the road. 'I can hear something! I think it's coming from over there.'

'That's the park,' Kitty told him. 'It's quite big, with a lake and a playground.'

The night breeze lifted the leaves on the trees, making them flutter. Kitty worked hard to use all her super senses. There was a strange rustling sound—too loud to be the wind—and an odd smell drifted over the park wall, like mud mixed with chocolate.

'Let's get a little closer. But we should be careful. This dog is acting very strangely,' Kitty said.

The park gate was locked, so Kitty climbed the high wall and pulled Ozzy up beside her. The owl boy crouched on the brick wall, moving his head slowly from side to side as he scanned the bushes and trees.

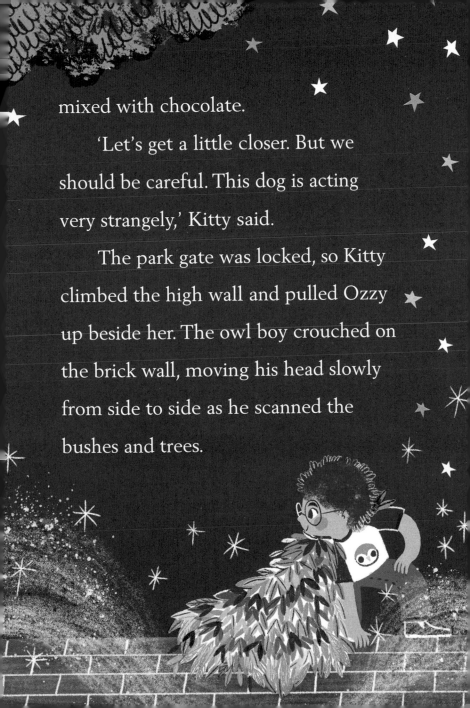

The park was full of cracklings and rustlings, and tree shadows stretched across the grass like long crooked fingers. The lake at the centre of the trees glinted as the moon came out from behind a cloud.

'I don't like this,'
quavered Pumpkin.
'Stay here!'
Kitty told the kitten.
'I'll call you when we
know it's safe.'

Pumpkin nodded and settled on
the wall, curling his little ginger tail
around his body.

'Let's split up,' suggested Ozzy.
'Olive and I will head to the other side
of the lake. Whoever finds the dog first
can call the others.'

56

'Good idea!' Kitty sprang down and crept through the undergrowth with Katsumi close behind her. Ozzy spread his cape wide and glided away through the trees.

'I'll check this way, Kitty,' whispered Katsumi, pointing to a small path that led away to the left.

Kitty nodded and tiptoed on a little further. Her cat-like powers let her move noiselessly through the bushes and her special night-time vision helped her notice every tiny movement.

A-ROOOO! A howl filled the air and the sad, lonely noise made Kitty shiver. Who was this strange, wild dog and what was he doing all alone in the dark?

Chapter
4

Kitty followed a trail of
broen branches that led across the grass.
Then she climbed a tall tree, hoping to
get a better view of the
park. A sudden growling noise came
from the middle of a bramble patch,

and Kitty spotted something in the shadows, roaming backwards and forwards.

Kitty shivered. The shadowy shape looked huge and monster-like. Then she reminded herself what her mum always said: *Remember, Kitty, you're braver than you think!*

Just as the shape came out of the bushes, a cloud hid the moon and the park sank into darkness. By the time Kitty focused with her night-time vision, the shape had disappeared.

Kitty was about to climb down from
the tree when she heard Katsumi.

'Kitty, over here!' Her friend's
voice came from high in the treetops.

Kitty ran along a branch and leapt
gracefully through the leaves. The wind
gusted strongly, but she balanced on the
swaying branch before somersaulting

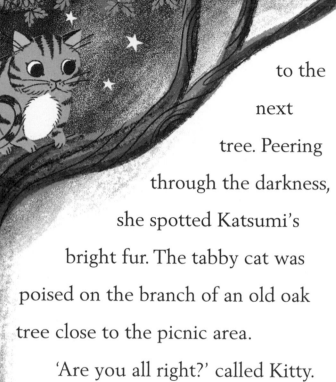

to the

next

tree. Peering

through the darkness,

she spotted Katsumi's

bright fur. The tabby cat was

poised on the branch of an old oak

tree close to the picnic area.

'Are you all right?' called Kitty.

'Yes, I'm fine,' replied Katsumi.

'The dog chased me up here—he

was quite terrifying.'

Kitty swiftly climbed across to her friend. 'Why is he acting like this? It makes no sense.'

Katsumi shook her head. 'He seems like a very strange creature! His eyes looked wild, and his coat was covered in twigs and leaves and big lumps of chocolate cake.'

'Did you talk to him?' asked Kitty.

'I tried to, but he drowned me out with his howling,' Katsumi told her. 'Then he chased me through the bushes. I escaped by climbing this tree, and I thought I'd wait here to see what he did next.'

'I'm going to get closer and see what he's doing.' Kitty climbed swiftly down the trunk and looked around.

The bushes were rustling on the other side of the picnic area, and there was a sharp whimpering sound.

Kitty crept across the grass past the picnic benches, her eyes fixed on the shaking bushes. The dog was thrashing wildly and breaking the branches.

Kitty's heart thumped, and she took a deep breath to try to stay calm.

'Stop right there!' she cried. 'My name is Kitty and I'm a superhero in training! Come out of that bush right now! You have a lot of explaining to do.'

The dog barked loudly and his thrashing grew even wilder. Leaves and twigs and bits of moss flew into the air. Kitty's eyes widened in alarm, and she got ready to leap out of the way in case the dog came charging straight at her.

At last the creature broke through the branches. Kitty jumped back, but the dog just slumped on the ground in

front of her with a whimper. 'I'm sorry!
I know I've been a bad, *bad* dog.'

'You've certainly had us chasing
all over the place to find you.' Kitty
hesitated. Then she crouched down
beside the creature. He was a beautiful

golden Labrador, but leaves and mud were stuck to his coat along with dollops of chocolate cream.

The dog gave a long groan and covered his eyes with one paw. Kitty saw his tail drooping and felt sorry for him in spite of all the trouble he'd caused. 'I'm Kitty,' she told him again. 'What's your name?'

'I'm Ludo and I live at the Sticky Bun Bakery. The humans that live there came to the stray animal home and picked me to be their dog. They're really nice to me and . . .' He broke off with a sob.

Kitty looked at him in surprise. 'If you like it there, why did you make such a mess?'

Ludo broke into another howl and Kitty patted his head. 'Shh! Why don't you tell me what's wrong? Maybe I can help.'

'They brought me a shiny leather collar with the bakery address and telephone number written in gold letters,' cried Ludo. 'But it's a bit loose and it must have come off somewhere!'

He sniffed before carrying on.

'I looked all over the shop and the bakery kitchen, but I couldn't find it. Then I came out here because this is where we came for a walk today!' He jumped up and looked around wildly. 'It *must* be here somewhere! I can't go back without it or my owners will think I don't

want to be their dog after all.' He began scrabbling at the earth and the bushes, covering both of them in twigs and leaves.

'Stop! I'll help you find it—I promise,' Kitty told him. 'We can look together.'

Ludo's sad eyes lit up. 'Really? You don't mind helping me?'

Kitty smiled. 'Of course not. My friends will help too.' Katsumi stepped gracefully through the bushes. 'Katsumi—this is Ludo and he's sad because he lost the collar his new owners gave him. I told him we'd help.'

Ludo looked ashamed. 'I'm sorry I chased you before! I was trying to explain, but everything came out wrong.'

'That's all right.' Katsumi turned to Kitty. 'Maybe we should call Ozzy and Olive.'

'Good idea.' Kitty looked around. Where was Ozzy? She hadn't seen him since they split up to search in different directions.

Just then, there was a clear hooting sound. *Tu-WIT! Tu-WOO!*

'That must be Ozzy,' explained Kitty. 'Let's go and meet him. His owl-powers give him brilliant eyesight so he'll be really helpful for finding your collar.'

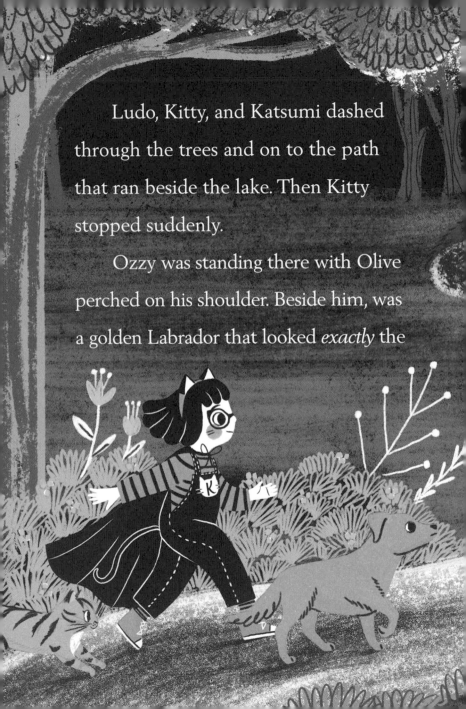

Ludo, Kitty, and Katsumi dashed through the trees and on to the path that ran beside the lake. Then Kitty stopped suddenly.

Ozzy was standing there with Olive perched on his shoulder. Beside him, was a golden Labrador that looked *exactly* the

same as Ludo. Except this dog was also
wearing a shiny leather collar.

Chapter 5

Ozzy grinned widely. 'I've found the dog from the bakery. His name is Tully and he's sorry he made such a mess . . .' He broke off, staring at Ludo. 'Who's that?'

Ludo sprang at Tully, barking

loudly. 'That's my collar! Give it back!'

Kitty pulled Ludo away. 'Wait a minute—*this* is the dog from the bakery,' she said to Ozzy. 'He's been running around looking for his lost collar.'

Ozzy looked from Ludo to Tully and frowned.

'That's not true! It's my collar,' said Tully. 'I'm the one that lives in the bakery and this dog is just fibbing!'

Ozzy's frown cleared. 'See! This is the bakery dog. Maybe this other one got into the shop and caused all the mess because he was hungry.'

Kitty looked into Ludo's sad brown eyes. She felt a tingling—like an extra sense—that what he'd told her was true. He would never have been so upset about losing the collar if it was all a lie.

'I know it's confusing, but I'm *sure* that Ludo is the real bakery dog,' she began.

'I don't think so!' Ozzy folded his arms. 'Your dog doesn't even have a collar. He's probably a stray.'

'I did have a collar,' howled Ludo. 'Then I lost it!'

Kitty folded her arms too. 'Actually, he's explained it all to

me—how his collar was loose and how he's worried his owners might be upset that he's lost it. I really believe him!'

'You're so sure you're right all the time!' Ozzy looked cross. 'You're not the only one with superpowers any more, you know.'

Kitty went red. It was really Ozzy that was acting like *he* was right all the time. 'This is silly! There's no point arguing about it . . .' She stared at the two dogs, her forehead creasing.

Pumpkin scampered up and brushed against Kitty's legs. 'What's happening? I heard all the shouting and thought I should come and help.' He looked nervously at the two dogs.

Olive ruffled her feathers. 'Both these dogs are saying they belong at the bakery. But one of them must be making it up.'

'If only there was a way to tell which one.' Katsumi swished her tail thoughtfully.

Kitty gazed at Tully's collar. The leather looked new and shiny, and the bakery's name, address and telephone 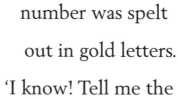 number was spelt out in gold letters. 'I know! Tell me the

82

phone number of the bakery written on that collar.'

Tully stuck his nose in the air. 'I don't know. I never read it!'

Ludo wagged his tail. 'That's easy!' And he reeled off the number perfectly.

Ozzy leaned closer to read the collar before glaring at Tully. 'You haven't been telling the truth!'

Tully laughed nastily. 'Who cares? We look the same and the owners of the bakery will never tell the difference.' He leapt out of Ozzy's reach with a growl. 'He's not getting the collar back! He shouldn't have lost it in the first place.'

'That's really mean!' Ozzy made a grab for Tully, but he darted out of the way again.

'No, it's not!' the dog snapped
back. 'Why should he get the chance
to live in that nice cosy place instead of
me?' Then he galloped away across the
park and disappeared behind the trees.

'Don't let him get away!'
howled Ludo.

'Don't worry—we can stop him,' Kitty said. 'But it's going to take teamwork.'

Ozzy nodded. 'Let's spread out and cover different sides of the park. Olive and I can go to the main gate.'

'That's a good idea!' said Kitty. 'Katsumi and Ludo, you cover the exit near the corner shop. Pumpkin and I will go to the left-hand corner where there's a gap in the fence. Together, we'll catch him!'

They raced away through the trees.

Kitty ran faster than ever, leaping over benches and bushes. She stopped by the gap in the fence, all her superpowers on full alert. Pumpkin crouched beside her. Kitty heard a tree creaking in the wind. Then a mouse scuttled through the fallen leaves.

Suddenly, there was a scuffling noise from the direction of the lake, followed by three

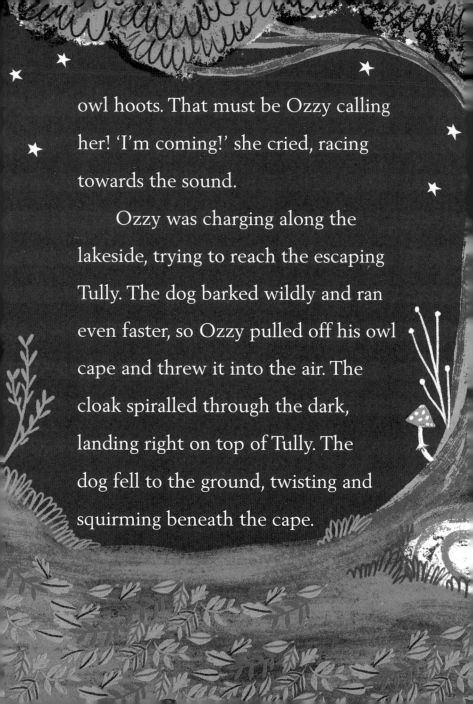

owl hoots. That must be Ozzy calling her! 'I'm coming!' she cried, racing towards the sound.

Ozzy was charging along the lakeside, trying to reach the escaping Tully. The dog barked wildly and ran even faster, so Ozzy pulled off his owl cape and threw it into the air. The cloak spiralled through the dark, landing right on top of Tully. The dog fell to the ground, twisting and squirming beneath the cape.

Ozzy dusted his hands together, proudly. 'I caught him! Now we can get that collar back.'

Just then, Tully wrenched himself free. Ozzy leapt back in surprise, and Tully staggered forwards, tumbling over the bank into the lake with a huge splash. 'Help, I can't swim!'

He thrashed around in the water.

　　Kitty sprang forward, but the dog had already floated out of reach. 'Don't worry! I'll get you.' She swung herself into a tree and darted along a branch that hung over the water. Reaching down, she grabbed Tully's collar and hauled him out of the lake. The dog fell

on to the bank, shivering, and looking very sorry for himself.

Kitty leapt to the ground and undid the collar, before giving it to Ludo. Then she took off her cape and wrapped it around Tully to stop him shivering.

Tully sniffed and looked at Ludo sadly. 'I know I shouldn't have kept the collar . . . but I wanted a home of my own so badly! When I saw you out for a walk with your owners I wished it was me—with a good home and people that love me! Then I saw the collar on the ground . . . and I took it.'

'I'm sorry you've been lonely.' Kitty crouched down beside him. 'Ozzy and I are superheroes in training, so maybe we could help?'

'Everyone deserves a good home,'

added Ludo, eagerly. 'It was the stray animal centre that helped me to find one. They're very nice people!'

'That's a wonderful idea!' said Kitty. 'We can take you to see them tonight.'

Tully jumped up and wagged his tail. Then he and Ludo touched noses.

'Sorry, Ludo,' said Tully.

'I'm glad we're friends now." Ludo wagged his tail too.

'So everything's sorted out at last,' said Pumpkin, stretching sleepily.

'It was so much easier when we worked together.'

Ozzy grinned at Kitty. 'I think we make quite a good team. Two superheroes are definitely better than one!'

Kitty smiled back. 'I think you're right!'

Chapter 6

Katsumi suggested cleaning the bakery before taking Tully to the animal centre, so they headed back there and worked hard to make the place perfect again. Olive picked up raisins with her beak while Katsumi

and Pumpkin pushed a cleaning cloth
around the worktops.

Ozzy mixed up some ingredients
and made a cake to replace the broken
one with the lemon-coloured icing.

'That looks delicious!' said Kitty admiringly.

'I really like making cakes,' Ozzy told her. 'It's a shame we can't try a bit of this one.'

'You could take some of these leftover cupcakes instead.' Ludo pointed to a row of cakes with swirly buttercream. 'I heard Mrs Gallo say they needed eating up!'

Kitty packed a few cupcakes into a paper bag and checked that the whole bakery was sparkling and clean.

Then they said goodbye to Ludo before walking down the road to the stray animal home.

Kitty knelt down beside Tully and hugged him gently. 'Good luck, Tully! I hope you can come and visit me once you've been given a new home.'

'Thank you for everything, and I'm sorry for the trouble I caused. I hope my new owners are kind like you two.' Tully touched noses with Kitty and then with Ozzy, before trotting through the gates of the animal centre.

Kitty sighed. 'I hope it doesn't take too long to find him a good owner. Everyone needs a place that feels like home.'

Ozzy nodded. 'Moving to Hallam City was really strange and scary. At first I didn't feel like I belonged here,

but now that I've found someone else
who's like me it's not such a bad place
after all!'

Kitty linked arms with him. 'Let's
go home and eat those cupcakes.'

By the time they reached the tree house, Kitty couldn't stop rubbing her tired eyes. She performed the final leap across to the old oak tree with Pumpkin lying on her shoulders already fast asleep. Olive's wings drooped as she perched on the windowsill of the tree house, and even Katsumi was yawning widely.

Kitty pulled the duvet over her legs, handing a cupcake to Ozzy.

'I think that was a job well done!' she said. 'Ludo got his collar back and now Tully has the chance for a home of his own.'

Ozzy took a bite
of cake. 'So tell me about
your other adventures, Kitty.'

'Only if you tell me yours too!'
said Kitty, grinning.

So Kitty told Ozzy all about her
cat crew and the adventures they often
had together by the light of the moon.
Then Ozzy told her about the little
village where he'd lived and all the owl
friends he'd made there.

'I'd like to get to know more of
the owls that live here in the city.'

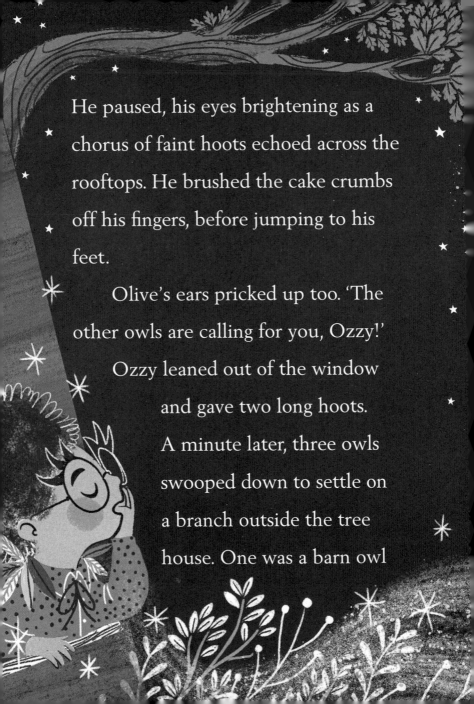

He paused, his eyes brightening as a chorus of faint hoots echoed across the rooftops. He brushed the cake crumbs off his fingers, before jumping to his feet.

Olive's ears pricked up too. 'The other owls are calling for you, Ozzy!'

Ozzy leaned out of the window and gave two long hoots. A minute later, three owls swooped down to settle on a branch outside the tree house. One was a barn owl

with a round white face and brown
feathers, the second was a tawny owl
with speckled wings, and the last one
was a long-eared owl with wide yellow
eyes.

'Then it's true-hoo,' said the barn
owl. 'A boy with owl-like powers has
come to Hallam City!'

'We heard all about your adventure in the park,' hooted the tawny owl.

'We're very good at silent flying and we'd love to help you on your next night-time mission,' added the long-eared owl.

Ozzy flushed happily. 'I'd love that too!'

'Now you'll have your own owl squad, just like my cat crew,' said Kitty, beaming.

The owls settled down to roost on the roof of the tree house while Kitty snuggled down with Katsumi and Pumpkin. The stars twinkled in the velvet-black sky and the wind gently rustled the leaves of the oak tree.

Kitty sighed happily and closed her eyes. Having superpowers was amazing fun, but it was going to be even better now she had someone to share it with!

Super Facts About Cats

Super Speed

Have you ever seen a cat make a quick escape from a dog? If so, you'll know that they can move *really* fast—up to 30mph!

Super Hearing

Cats have an incredible sense of hearing and can swivel their large ears to pinpoint even the tiniest of sounds.

Super Reflexes

Have you ever heard the saying 'cats always land on their feet'? People say this because cats have amazing reflexes. If a cat is falling, they can sense quickly how to move their bodies into the right position to land safely.

Super Leaps

A cat can jump over eight feet high
in a single leap; this is due to its powerful
back leg muscles.

Super Vision

Cats have amazing night-time vision. Their
incredible ability to see in low light allows them
to hunt for prey when it's dark outside.

Super Smell

Cats have a very powerful sense of smell,
14 times stronger than a human's. Did you know
that the pattern of ridges on each cat's nose
is as unique as a human's fingerprint?

Kitty

and the
Moonlight Rescue

Girl by day. Cat by night. Ready for adventure

Written by **Paula Harrison** • *Illustrated by* **Jenny Løvlie**

Here's a taste of what's to come . . .

Kitty's family is extra special—Mum is a superhero and Kitty knows that one day she'll use her special powers to be a hero too.

That day comes sooner than expected when Figaro the cat comes to her bedroom window to ask for help. But the world at night is a scary place—is Kitty brave enough to step out into the darkness for a thrilling moonlight adventure?

Kitty

and the
Tiger Treasure

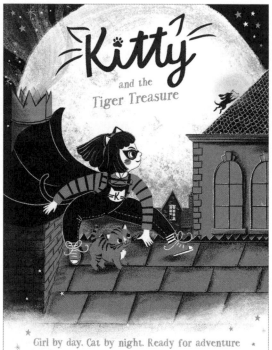

Girl by day. Cat by night. Ready for adventure

Written by Paula Harrison • *Illustrated by* Jenny Løvlie

Here's a taste of what's to come . . .

Kitty can't wait to visit the museum and see the priceless Golden Tiger Statue with her own eyes. Legend tells that those in possession of the statue can make their greatest wish come true . . .

Kitty can't resist a little night-time adventure to show Pumpkin the statue while there's no one else around, but disaster strikes when the statue is stolen and Kitty is accused of the crime.

Will Kitty clear her name, find the culprit, and return the precious statue before sunrise?

Kitty

and the
Sky Garden Adventure

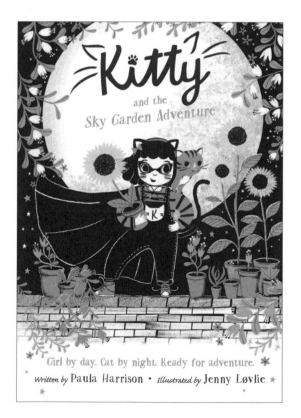

Kitty

and the
Sky Garden Adventure

Girl by day. Cat by night. Ready for adventure.

Written by Paula Harrison • Illustrated by Jenny Løvlie

Here's a taste of what's to come . . .

Kitty, Pumpkin, and Pixie discover a
secret sky garden on the city rooftops.

It's a wondrous place, filled with exotic plants
and beautiful decorations. Pixie is so excited that she
wants to tell the world about it, but the more cats that
learn of the secret garden, the wilder it becomes. Soon
Kitty has to step in to rescue the garden and its beauty
from those who seem intent on destroying it.

About the author

Paula Harrison

Before launching a successful writing career,
Paula was a primary school teacher. Her years teaching
taught her what children like in stories and how
they respond to humour and suspense. She went on
to put her experience to good use, writing many
successful stories for young readers.

About the illustrator

Jenny Løvlie

Jenny is a Norwegian illustrator, designer, creative, foodie and bird enthusiast. She is fascinated by the strong bond between humans and animals and loves using bold colours and shapes in her work.

Love Kitty?
Why not try these too . . .

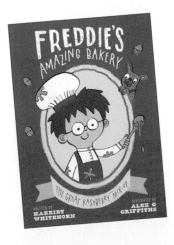